Everett Anderson's
Nine Month Long

Everett Anderson's Nine Month Long

by Lucille Clifton

illustrations by Ann Grifalconi

Holt, Rinehart and Winston • New York

10 9 8 7 6 5 4 3 2 1

Library of Congress Cataloging in Publication Data
Clifton, Lucille, 1936-
    Everett Anderson's nine month long.

    SUMMARY: A small boy and his family anticipate the birth
of their newest member.
    [1. Babies—Fiction. 2. Brothers and sisters—Fiction.
3. Stories in rhyme] I. Grifalconi, Ann. II. Title.
PZ8.3.C573Evk   [E]   78-4202   ISBN 0-03-043536-6
ISBN 0-03-043536-6

for Steve,
whenever—L.C.
for Danny, Jr.—A.G.

Mama is Mrs. Perry now, and it's fun
that Mr. Tom Perry is almost a dad
and doesn't mind that Everett Anderson
plans to keep the name he had.

"Whatever our names are
we know what we've got."
Mr. Perry smiles. "Love,
and that is a lot."

2

Mama is smiling in a new way
and Mr. Perry is humming and humming
and Everett Anderson thinks that they
act as if something special is coming.

3

"Everett Anderson, you are a joy
to me, you are my own dear boy,

and we have so much love. We care
so much that we might have love to share,

and how do you feel about another
someone to love and be loved by—a brother

or sister? Everett, what do you say?"

Everett watches his mama all day

and just at bedtime whispers into her hair,
"Yes, I think there's enough love, it's okay to share."

4

Something is growing in 14A.
Something resting inside a place
warm and soft. His mama's face
is gentle. Everett likes to say
that if he were a baby again, he'd start
again just like that; near his mama's heart.

5

Mrs. Perry is sitting
and rocking and rocking
these days
and Everett sits beside her
and notices how his mama is smiling
and singing and spreading
wider and wider.

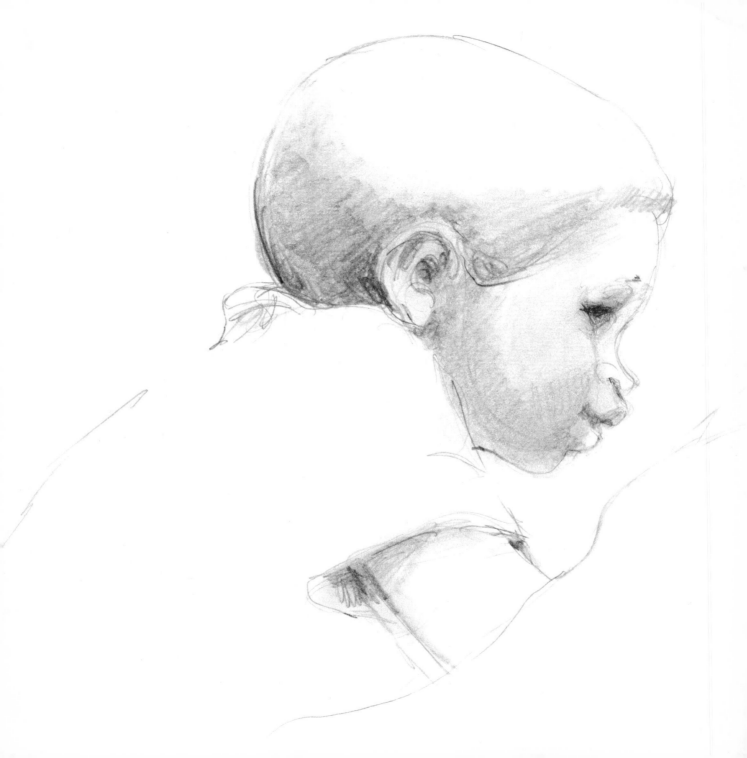

6

The baby,
maybe a sister and maybe a brother,
keeps knocking on Everett Anderson's mother.
"It wants to come out.
It wants to see."
Everett Anderson thinks,
"It wants to laugh and play with me."

7

"When we were just two"
—Everett Anderson frowns—
"Mama would play with me
and now
she hardly can run
or fly a kite
and has to rest
both day and night
and hardly even spanks me now.
It seems Mr. Perry's fault somehow."

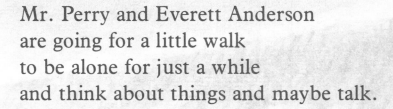

8

Mr. Perry and Everett Anderson
are going for a little walk
to be alone for just a while
and think about things and maybe talk.

"My mama is different, I can see,"
Everett Anderson says.
"Well, I agree,"
says Mr. Perry, "but in our hearts
we know that she is still the same
mama who loves you whatever her name
and whatever other sister or brother.
You know you are her special one,
her firstborn Everett Anderson."

Everett and Mr. Perry smile
and hold hands together after a while.

9

Everybody in 14A
is waiting and waiting for the day
and Mr. Perry and Everett keep
worrying Mama with
"Do you need to sleep?"

Ladies and gentlemen,
hooray for us!
With just a little bit
of fuss
we would like to have
all of you meet
somebody brown and warm
and sweet
who has come to be part
of our family, too—
Baby Evelyn Perry says
— How Do You Do! —